Emma's
New Game

Written by Gerald Mercer

Illustrated by Jillian Nicol

Pennywell Books
St. John's
2009

Library and Archives Canada Cataloguing in Publication

Mercer, Gerald

    Emma's new game / written by Gerald Mercer ; illustrated by Jillian Nicol.

ISBN 978-1-897317-44-0

    I. Nicol, Jillian Eve, 1982–   II. Title.

PS8626.E74E44 2009   jC813'.6   C2009-904257-6

PRINTED IN CANADA

Pennywell Books is an imprint of Flanker Press Limited.

FLANKER PRESS
P.O. BOX 2522, STATION C
ST. JOHN'S, NL A1C 6K1 CANADA
TOLL-FREE: 1-866-739-4420
WWW.FLANKERPRESS.COM

COVER DESIGN AND BOOK LAYOUT: DWAYNE LAFITTE

14 13 12 11 10 09   1 2 3 4 5 6 7 8 9

Canada   Canada Council Conseil des Arts   Newfoundland
                  for the Arts   du Canada   Labrador

We acknowledge the financial support of: the Government of Canada through the Book Publishing Industry Development Program (BPIDP) for our publishing activities; the Canada Council for the Arts which last year invested $20.1 million in writing and publishing throughout Canada; the Government of Newfoundland and Labrador, Department of Tourism, Culture and Recreation.

To grandparents everywhere who have been energized by playing childhood games with their grandchildren.

GM

To those special people in my life whom I love and miss.

JN

In the garden behind Poppy T's shed, there stood a tall horse chestnut tree. Emma never really took any notice of it. She liked the shed and spent hours playing in it.

The summer was quickly turning to fall. Nanny T, Poppy T, and Emma were getting ready to go partridgeberry picking.

Inside the shed, Emma was trying on an old pair of workboots. "I'll wear these," she said. "They'll keep me dry."

Thump. Thump-thump. Something hit the roof and tumbled to the ground. Emma jumped up and darted to the doorway. Poppy T was coming to get his rubber boots.

"What was that?" Emma asked. "I heard a thump on the roof."

Poppy T went behind the shed and returned with a prickly green and brown pod. He wiggled his thumbs between the spines and peeled back the husk.

"There is a horse chestnut hiding inside," he said.

Emma's eyes were fixed on the chestnut. She did not notice her friends approaching.

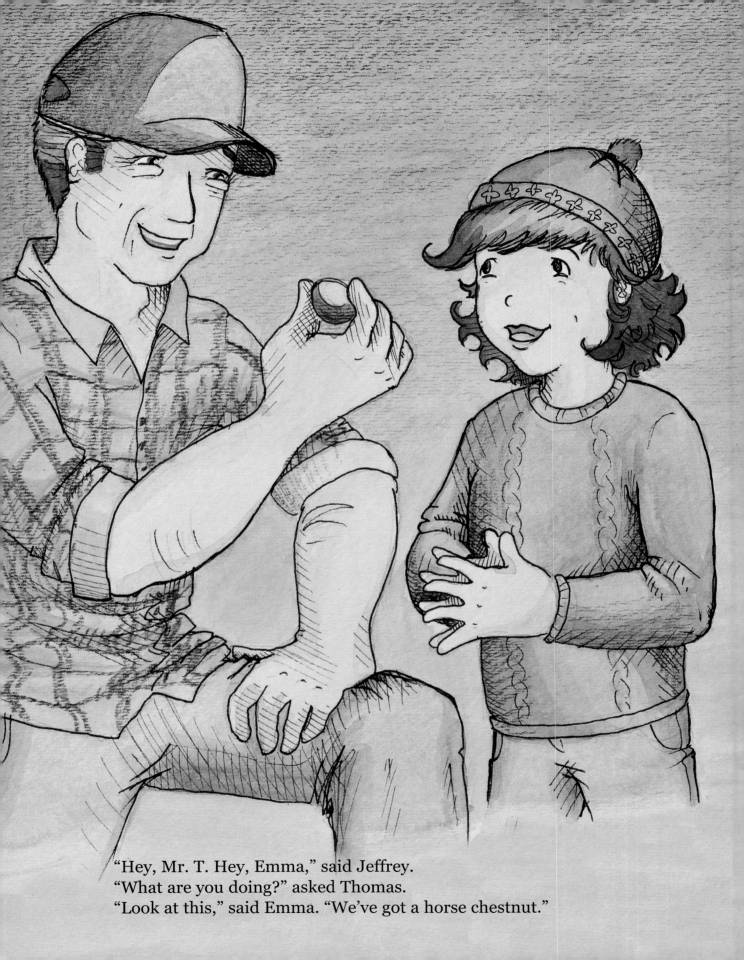

"Hey, Mr. T. Hey, Emma," said Jeffrey.
"What are you doing?" asked Thomas.
"Look at this," said Emma. "We've got a horse chestnut."

"Horse chestnuts are no good for eating," said Poppy T. "We used to play a game with them. We'd choose the best chestnuts, bake them in the oven, drill a hole through them and hang them on a string. Back then we called the game chestnuts. Today people call it conkers."

"How did you play?" asked Jeffrey.

"One fella would let his chestnut dangle on the end of the string. Then the other fella would swing his chestnut at it. If he hit it, he would get another turn. If he missed it, the other fella would let his chestnut dangle. The first person to smash the other fella's chestnut off the string won," explained Poppy T.

"The winning chestnut earned a title," Poppy T continued. "If both chestnuts were new, the winner became a one-er. If a new chestnut smashed a three-er, the winner became a four-er — one for the win plus the battles of the three-er. One plus three makes four. Get it?"

Thomas scratched his head. "So, if my chestnut was a two-er and it smashed your three-er, then . . ."

"Yours would be a six-er, because a two-er plus a three-er makes it a five-er and then you add one for winning the match," calculated Emma.

"You're right!" exclaimed Poppy T. "Would you like to make some?"

"Come on. Let's get some chestnuts!" Emma cried.

The children ran to the back of the shed. Poppy T grabbed a junk of wood and joined them.

"Stand back," Poppy T said. He threw the junk up into the tree. The branches rattled, and some pods fell. Thomas and Emma dove in to scoop them up.

"Ouch!" cried Thomas. "Those spikes hurt!"

"You have to be careful when you collect chestnuts," warned Poppy T.

Jeffrey picked up the junk and threw it up again. Pods tumbled off the roof and onto the ground. Emma, Thomas, and Jeffrey collected all they could.

Nanny T rounded the corner of the shed, berry buckets in hand. "Are you two ready to go berry picking?" she asked. "Oh, I see. Poppy T has been telling you about chestnuts. Thomas, your poppy used to be the champion on this shore. He knew how to choose the hardest chestnuts. And, Jeffrey, I remember your grandfather saying that he once owned a twelve-er."

"That means he won enough battles to add up to twelve, right?" asked Jeffrey, eyes flashing.

"That's right. Having a twelve-er made him a real champion," Nanny T said.

"I've got to go talk to my pop," said Jeffrey. He ran out of the garden. Thomas left, too, carrying a bunch of chestnuts in his hands.

Before turning to go back to the house, Nanny T said to Emma, "Here, take these buckets. You might need them. We can go berry picking later."

"Come on, Emma. We've got a job to do," said Poppy T.

Emma and her grandfather carefully gathered the horse chestnut pods,
placed them in the berry buckets and went back into the shed.

Poppy T peeled the chestnuts, examined each one and chose the best. The rest, Emma tossed onto the ground behind the shed.

"Let's go bake them," said Poppy T.

In the kitchen, Poppy T turned the oven on to very low heat.

Emma spread the chestnuts on a baking sheet, and

Poppy T placed the sheet on the middle rack in the oven.

After an hour, Poppy T turned off the oven. He put on an oven mitt and took out the baking sheet.

"These look pretty good," he said. Poppy T carefully removed the chestnuts and placed them in a berry bucket.

"What do we do now?" asked Emma.

Poppy T replied, "First we let them cool. Then we use a drill to put a hole through each of them."

In the shed, Poppy T drilled a hole through the centre of each chestnut.
Emma tossed out the ones that cracked and kept the good ones.

"Are you still wearing those old workboots, Emma?" asked Poppy T. "Take them off and give me the laces. We have conkers to make."

Emma removed the laces from the boots. Poppy T tied a knot at the end of each one. They strung a chestnut on each lace and let them dangle.

"Ready?" asked Emma.

"Ready," replied Poppy T. "You go first."

The match was on! Emma held the lace between the thumb and index finger of her left hand. She grasped the chestnut in her right hand and pulled it tight. Emma aimed her chestnut directly at the one dangling from Poppy T's lace.

She snapped her wrist and let go. The chestnut flew forward. It was a direct hit!

"Your turn again," said Poppy T.

This time, Emma missed. It was Poppy T's turn.

Poppy T pulled back on his lace. He took aim and . . .

"Mr. T, we've got conkers," exclaimed Jeffrey.

Poppy T and Emma looked up. Jeffrey and his grandfather stood in the doorway, each holding a chestnut on a string. Thomas and his grandfather were right behind them.

"Come in, b'ys. If you're here for a battle, you're on!" said Poppy T.

The children and their grandfathers challenged each other. Chestnuts flew off the ends of the strings. They laced new ones and discarded the cracked ones. In the end, there were just two contenders left, Emma and Uncle Sim, Thomas's grandfather. Emma had a seven-er and Uncle Sim had a four-er.

Emma and Uncle Sim took turns striking each other's chestnuts. Uncle Sim's chestnut started to crack. Emma took aim and let her chestnut fly. It struck Uncle Sims's chestnut and shattered it to bits!

"What's going on here?" asked Nanny T, as she and the two other grandmothers approached the shed. "You children ought to come in for tea and pie."

Emma, Thomas, Jeffrey, and their grandparents headed for the house. Emma clutched her conker and smiled. She looked at Poppy T and said proudly, "Mine's a twelve-er."

Poppy T gave Emma a big hug. "You're the new champion on this shore."

ABOUT THE AUTHOR

GERALD N. J. MERCER has been an educator in Newfoundland and Labrador for twenty-eight years. He remembers walking to and from school in the fall, filling his pockets with horse chestnuts that had fallen from neighbourhood trees. Although he tried many different ways of preparing them for battle, the oven method seemed to work best. Gerald Mercer lives with his wife, Daphne, and three children, Rebecca, Andrew, and Simeon, in Mount Pearl, Newfoundland and Labrador.

ABOUT THE ILLUSTRATOR

JILLIAN NICOL was born and raised in St. John's, Newfoundland. Always a lover of art, she attended Sir Wilfred Grenfell University and obtained a BFA in Visual Art. After finishing school, she worked in St. John's as a screen printer, t-shirt designer, and freelance illustrator, a career she is working hard to pursue in her current home of Gatineau, Quebec.